DATE DUE

BCD	
	DISCARD
GAYLORD	PRINTED IN U.S.A.

The Ballad of

BALLARD
AND
SANDRINE

The Ballad of

BALLARD
AND
SANDRINE

PETER STRAUB

SUBTERRANEAN PRESS 2011

First Edition

ISBN
978-1-59606-441-6

Subterranean Press
PO Box 190106
Burton, MI 48519

www.subterraneanpress.com

Previously publishd in *Conjunctions.*

{ 1997

S o, do we get lunch again today?" Ballard asked. They had reached the steaming, humid end of November.

"We got fucking lunch yesterday," replied the naked woman splayed on the long table: knees bent, one hip elevated, one boneless-looking arm draped along the curves of her body, which despite its hidden scars appeared to be at least a decade younger than her face. "Why should today be different?"

After an outwardly privileged childhood polluted by parental misconduct, a superior education, and two failed marriages, Sandrine Loy had evolved into a rebellious, still-exploratory woman of forty. At present, her voice had a well-honed edge, as if she were explaining something to a person of questionable intelligence.

Two days before joining Sandrine on this river journey, Ballard had celebrated his sixty-fifth birthday at a dinner in Hong Kong, one of the cities where he conducted his odd business. Sandrine had not been invited to the dinner and would not have attended if she had. The formal, ceremonious side of Ballard's life, which he found so satisfying, interested her not at all.

Without in any way adjusting the facts of the extraordinary body she had put on display, Sandrine lowered her eyes from the ceiling and examined him with a glance brimming with false curiosity and false innocence. The glance also contained a flicker of genuine irritation.

Abruptly and with vivid recall, Ballard found himself remembering the late afternoon in 1969 when, nine floors above Park Avenue, upon a carpet of almost unutterable richness in a room hung with paintings by Winslow Homer and Albert Pinkham Ryder, he had stood with a rich scapegrace and client named Lauritzen Loy, his host, to greet Loy's daughter on her return from another grueling day at Dalton School, then observed the sidelong, graceful, slightly miffed entrance of a fifteen-year-old girl in pigtails and a Jackson

Brown sweatshirt two sizes too large, met her gray-green eyes, and felt the very shape of his universe alter in some drastic way, either expanding a thousand times or contracting to a pinpoint, he could not tell. The second their eyes met, the girl blushed, violently.

She hadn't liked that, not at all.

"I didn't say it was going to be different, and I don't think it will." He turned to look at her, making sure to meet her gaze before letting his eye travel down her neck, over her breasts, the bowl of her belly, the slope of her pubis, the length of her legs. "Are you in a more than ordinarily bad mood?"

"You're snapping at me."

Ballard sighed. "You gave me that *look*. You said, 'Why should today be different?'"

"Have it your way, old man. But as a victory, it's fucking pathetic. It's hollow."

She rolled onto her back and gave her body a firm little shake that settled it more securely onto the steel surface of the table. The metal, only slightly cooler than her skin, felt good against it. In this climate, nothing not on ice or in a freezer, not even a corpse, could ever truly get cold.

"Most victories are hollow, believe me."

Ballard wandered over to the brass-bound porthole on the deck side of their elaborate, many-roomed suite. Whatever he saw caused him momentarily to stiffen and take an involuntary step backwards.

"What's the view like?"

"The so-called view consists of the filthy Amazon and a boring, muddy bank. Sometimes the bank is so far away it's out of sight."

He did not add that a Ballard approximately twenty years younger, the Ballard of, say, 1976, dressed in a handsome dark suit and brilliantly white shirt, was leaning against the deck rail, unaware of being under the eye of his twenty-years-older self. Young Ballard, older Ballard observed, did an excellent job of concealing his dire internal condition beneath a mask of deep, already well-weathered urbanity: the same performance, enacted day after day before an audience unaware of being an audience and never permitted backstage.

Unlike Sandrine, Ballard had never married. "Poor Ballard, stuck on the *Endless Night* with a horrible view and only his aging, moody girlfriend for company."

PETER STRAUB

Smiling, he returned to the long steel table, ran his mutilated right hand over the curve of her belly, and cupped her navel. "This is exactly what I asked for. You're wonderful."

"But isn't it funny to think—everything could have been completely different."

Ballard slid the remaining fingers of his hand down to palpate, lightly, the springy black shrub-like curls of her pubic bush.

"Everything is completely different right now."

"So take off your clothes and fuck me," Sandrine said. "I can get you hard again in a minute. In thirty seconds."

"I'm sure you could. But maybe you should put some clothes *on*, so we could go into lunch."

"You prefer to have sex in our bed."

"I do, yes. I don't understand why you wanted to get naked and lie down on this thing, anyhow. Now, I mean."

"It isn't cold, if that's what you're afraid of." She wriggled her torso and did a snow angel movement with her legs.

"Maybe this time we could catch the waiters."

"Because we'd be early?"

Ballard nodded. "Indulge me. Put on that sleeveless white French thing."

"Aye, aye, *mon capitain*." She sat up and scooted down the length of the table, pushing herself along on the raised vertical edges. These were of dark green marble, about an inch thick and four inches high. On both sides, round metal drains abutted the inner side of the marble. At the end of the table, Sandrine swung her legs down and straightened her arms, like a girl sitting on the end of a diving board. "I know why, too."

"Why I want you to wear that white thing? I love the way it looks on you."

"Why you don't want to have sex on this table."

"It's too narrow."

"You're thinking about what this table is for. Right? And you don't want to combine sex with *that*. Only I think that's exactly why we *should* have sex here."

"Everything we do, remember, is done by mutual consent. Our Golden Rule."

"Golden Spoilsport," she said. "Golden Shower of Shit."

PETER STRAUB

"See? Everything's different already."

Sandrine levered herself off the edge of the table and faced him like a strict schoolmistress who happened momentarily to be naked. "I'm all you've got, and sometimes even I don't understand you."

"That makes two of us."

She wheeled around and padded into the bedroom, displaying her plush little bottom and sacral dimples with an absolute confidence Ballard could not but admire.

Although Sandrine and Ballard burst, in utter defiance of a direct order, into the dining room a full nine minutes ahead of schedule, the unseen minions had already done their work and disappeared. On the gleaming rosewood table two formal place settings had been laid, the plates topped with elaborately chased silver covers. Fresh irises brushed blue and yellow filled a tall, sparkling crystal vase.

"I swear, they must have a greenhouse on this yacht," Ballard said.

"Naked men with muddy hair row the flowers out in the middle of the night."

"I don't even think irises grow in the Amazon basin."

"Little guys who speak bird-language can probably grow anything they like."

"That's only one tribe, the Piraha. And all those bird-sounds are actual words. It's a human language." Ballard walked around the table and took the seat he had claimed as his. He lifted the intricate silver cover. "Now what is that?" He looked across at Sandrine, who was prodding at the contents of her bowl with a fork.

"Looks like a cut-up sausage. At least I hope it's a sausage. And something like broccoli. And a lot of orangey-yellowy goo." She raised her fork and licked the tines. "Um. Tastes pretty good, actually. But…."

For a moment, she appeared to be lost in time's great forest.

"I know this doesn't make sense, but if we ever did this before, *exactly* this, with you sitting over there and me here, in this same room, well, wasn't the food even better, I mean a *lot* better?"

"I can't say anything about that," Ballard said. "I really can't. There's just this vague…." The vagueness disturbed him far more than seemed quite rational. "Let's drop that subject and talk about bird language. Yes, let's. And the wine."

PETER STRAUB

He picked up the bottle. "Yet again a very nice Bordeaux," Ballard said, and poured for both of them. "However. What you've been hearing are real birds, not the Piraha."

"But they're talking, not just chirping. There's a difference. These guys are saying things to each other."

"Birds talk to one another. I mean, they sing."

She was right about one thing, though: in a funky, down-home way, the stew-like dish was delicious. He thrust away the feeling that it should have been a hundred, a thousand times more delicious: that once it, or something rather like it, had been paradisal.

"Birds don't sing in sentences. Or in paragraphs, like these guys do."

"They still can't be the Piraha. The Piraha live about five hundred miles away, on the Peruvian border."

"Your ears aren't as good as mine. You don't really hear them."

"Oh, I hear plenty of birds. They're all over the place."

"Only we're not talking about *birds*," Sandrine said.

{1982

*O*n the last day of November, Sandrine Loy, who was twenty-five, constitutionally ill-tempered, and startlingly good-looking (wide eyes, long mouth, black widow's peak, columnar legs), formerly of Princeton and Clare College, Cambridge, glanced over her shoulder and said, "Please tell me you're kidding. I just showered. I put on this nice white frock you bought me in Paris. And I'm *hungry*." Relenting a bit, she let a playful smile warm her face for nearly a second. "Besides that, I want to catch sight of our invisible servants."

"I'm hungry, too."

"Not for food, unfortunately." She spun from the porthole and its ugly view—a mile of brown, rolling river and low, muddy banks where squat, sullen natives tended to melt back into the bushes when the *Sweet Delight* went by—to indicate the evidence of Ballard's arousal, which stood up, darker than the rest of him, as straight as a flagpole.

"Let's have sex on this table. It's a lot more comfortable than it looks."

"Kind of defeats the fucking purpose, wouldn't you say? Comfort's hardly the point."

"Might as well be as comfy as we can, I say." He raised his arms to let his hands drape from the four-inch marble edging on the long steel table. "There's plenty of space on this thing, you know. More than in your bed at Clare."

"Maybe you're not as porky as I thought you were."

"Careful, careful. If you insult me, I'll make you pay for it."

At fifty, Ballard had put on some extra weight, but it suited him. His shoulders were still wider than his hips, and his belly more nascent than actual. His hair, longer than that of most men his age and just beginning to show threads of gray within the luxuriant brown, framed his wide brow and executive face. He looked like an actor who had made a career of playing senators, doctors,

PETER STRAUB

and bankers. Ballard's real profession was that of
fixer to an oversized law firm in New York with
a satellite office in Hong Kong, where he had
grown up. The weight of muscle in his arms,
shoulders, and legs reinforced the hint of stubborn
determination, even perhaps brutality in his face:
the suggestion that if necessary he would go a
great distance and perform any number of grim
deeds to do what was needed. Scars both long
and short, scars like snakes, zippers, and tattoos
bloomed here and there on his body.

"Promises, promises," she said. "But just for
now, get up and get dressed, please. The sight of
you admiring your own dick doesn't do anything
for me."

"Oh, really?"

"Well, I do like the way you can still stick
straight up into the air like a happy little soldier—
at your age! But men are so soppy about their
penises. You're all queer for yourselves. You more
so than most, Ballard."

"Ouch," he said, and sat up. "I believe I'll put
my clothes on now, Sandrine."

"Don't take forever, all right? I know it's only
the second day, but I'd like to get a look at them

while they're setting the table. Because someone, maybe even two someones, does set that table."

Ballard was already in the bedroom, pulling from their hangers a pair of white linen slacks and a thick, long-sleeved white cotton T-shirt. In seconds, he had slipped into these garments and was sliding his sun-tanned feet into rope-soled clogs.

"So let's move," he said, coming out of the bedroom with a long stride, his elbows bent, his forearms raised.

From the dining room came the sharp, distinctive chirping of a bird. Two notes, the second one higher, both clear and as insistent as the call of a bell. Ballard glanced at Sandrine, who seemed momentarily shaken.

"I'm not going in there if one of those awful jungle birds got in. They have to get rid of it. We're paying them, aren't we?"

"You have no idea," Ballard said. He grabbed her arm and pulled her along with him. "But that's no bird, it's *them*. The waiters. The staff."

Sandrine's elegant face shone with both disbelief and disgust.

"Those chirps and whistles are how they talk. Didn't you hear them last night and this morning?"

PETER STRAUB

When he pulled again at her arm, she followed along, reluctance visible in her stance, her gait, the tilt of her head.

"I'm talking about birds, and they weren't even on the yacht. They were on shore. They were up in the air."

"Let's see what's in here." Six or seven minutes remained until the official start of dinner time, and they had been requested never to enter the dining room until the exact time of the meal.

Ballard threw the door open and pulled her into the room with him. Silver covers rested on the Royal Doulton china, and an uncorked bottle of a distinguished Bordeaux stood precisely at the mid-point between the two place settings. Three inches to its right, a navy-blue-and-royal-purple orchid thick enough to eat leaned, as if languishing, against the side of a small square crystal vase. The air seemed absolutely unmoving. Through the thumb holes at the tops of the plate covers rose a dense, oddly meaty odor of some unidentifiable food.

"Missed 'em again, damn it." Sandrine pulled her arm from Ballard's grasp and moved a few steps away.

"But you have noticed that there's no bird in here. Not so much as a feather."

"So it got out—I know it was here, Ballard."

She spun on her four-inch heels, giving the room a fast 360-degree inspection. Their dining room, roughly oval in shape, was lined with glassed-in bookshelves of dark-stained oak containing perhaps five hundred books, most of them mid-to-late nineteenth and early twentieth century novels ranked alphabetically by author, regardless of genre. The jackets had been removed, which Ballard minded, a bit. Three feet in front of the bookshelves on the deck side, which yielded space to two portholes and a door, stood a long wooden table with a delicately inlaid top—a real table, unlike the one in the room they had just left, which was more like a work station in a laboratory. The real one was presumably for setting out buffets.

The first door opened out onto the deck; another at the top of the oval led to their large and handsomely-furnished sitting room, with reading chairs and lamps, two sofas paired with low tables, a bar with a great many bottles of liquor, two red lacquered cabinets they had as yet not explored, and an air of many small precious things set out

PETER STRAUB

to gleam under the parlor's low lighting. The two remaining doors in the dining room were on the interior side. One opened into the spacious corridor that ran the entire length of their suite and gave access to the deck on both ends; the other revealed a gray passageway and a metal staircase that led up to the Captain's deck and cabin and down into the engine room, galley, and quarters for the yacht's small, unseen crew.

"So it kept all its feathers," said Sandrine. "If you don't think that's possible, you don't know doodly-squat about birds."

"What isn't possible," said Ballard, "is that some giant parrot got out of here without opening a door or a porthole."

"One of the waiters let it out, dummy. One of those handsome *Spanish-speaking* waiters."

They sat on opposite sides of the stately table. Ballard smiled at Sandrine, and she smiled back in rage and distrust. Suddenly and without warning, he remembered the girl she had been on Park Avenue at the end of the sixties, gawky-graceful, brilliantly surly, her hair and wardrobe goofy, claiming him as he had claimed her, with a glance. He had rescued her father from ruinous shame and a long jail term, but as soon as he had seen her he understood that his work had just begun, and that it would demand restraint, sacrifice, patience, and adamantine caution.

"A three-count?" he asked.

She nodded.

"One," he said. "Two." They put their thumbs into the round holes at the tops of the covers. "Three." They raised their covers, releasing steam and smoke and a more concentrated, powerful form of the meaty odor.

"Wow. What is that?"

Yellow-brown sauce or gravy covered a long, curved strip of foreign matter. Exhausted vegetables that looked a little like okra and string beans but were other things altogether lay strewn in limp surrender beneath the gravy.

"All of a sudden I'm really hungry," said Sandrine. "You can't tell what it is, either?"

Ballard moved the strip of unknown meat back and forth with his knife. Then he jabbed his fork into it. A watery yellow fluid oozed from the punctures.

"God knows what this is."

He pictured some big reptilian creature sliding down the riverbank into the meshes of a native net, then being hauled back up to be pierced with poison-tipped wooden spears. Chirping like birds, the diminutive men rioted in celebration around the corpse, which was now that of a hideous insect the size of a pony, its shell a poisonous green.

"I'm not even sure it's a mammal," he said. "Might even be some organ. Anaconda liver. Crocodile lung. Tarantula heart."

"You first."

Ballard sliced a tiny section from the curved meat before him. He half-expected to see valves and tubes, but the slice was a dense light brown all the way through. Ballard inserted the morsel into his mouth, and his taste buds began to sing.

"My god. Amazing."

"It's good?"

"Oh, this is way beyond 'good.'"

Ballard cut a larger piece off the whole and quickly bit into it. Yes, there it was again, but more sumptuous, almost floral in its delicacy and grounded in some profoundly satisfactory flavor, like that of a great single-barrel bourbon laced with a dark, subversive French chocolate. Subtlety, strength, sweetness. He watched Sandrine lift a section of the substance on her fork and slip it into her mouth. Her face went utterly still, and her eyes narrowed. With luxuriant slowness, she began to chew. After perhaps a second, Sandrine closed her eyes. Eventually, she swallowed.

"Oh, yes," she said. "My, my. Yes. Why can't we eat like this at home?"

"Whatever kind of animal this is, it's probably unknown everywhere but here. People like J. Paul Getty might get to eat it once a year, at some secret location."

"I don't care what it is, I'm just extraordinarily happy that we get to have it today. It's even a little bit sweet, isn't it?"

A short time later, Sandrine said, "Amazing. Even these horrible-looking vegetables spill out amazing flavors. If I could eat like this every day, I'd be perfectly happy to live in a hut, walk around barefoot, bathe in the Amazon, and wash my rags on the rocks."

"I know exactly what you mean," said Ballard. "It's like a drug. Maybe it is a drug."

"Do the natives really eat this way? Whatever this animal was, before they serve it to us, they have to hunt it down and kill it. Wouldn't they keep half of it for themselves?"

PETER STRAUB

"Be a temptation," Ballard said. "Maybe they lick our plates, too."

"Tell me the truth now, Ballard. If you know it. Okay?"

Chewing, he looked up into her eyes. Some of the bliss faded from his face. "Sure. Ask away."

"Did we ever eat this stuff before?"

Ballard did not answer. He sliced a quarter sized piece off the meat and began to chew, his eyes on his plate.

"I know I'm not supposed to ask."

He kept chewing and chewing until he swallowed. He sipped his wine. "No. Isn't that strange? How we know we're not supposed to do certain things?"

"Like see the waiters. Or the maids, or the Captain."

"Especially the Captain, I think."

"Let's not talk anymore, let's just eat for a little while."

Sandrine and Ballard returned to their plates and glasses, and for a time made no noise other than soft moans of satisfaction.

When they had nearly finished, Sandrine said, "There are so many books on this boat! It's like a big library. Do you think you've ever read one?"

"Do you?"

"I have the feeling...well, of course that's the reason I'm asking. In a way, I mean in a *real* way, we've never been here before. On the Amazon? Absolutely not. My husband, besides being continuously unfaithful, is a total asshole who never pays me any attention at all unless he's angry with me, but he's also tremendously jealous and possessive. For me to get here to be with you required an amazing amount of secret organization. D-Day didn't take any more planning than this trip. On the other hand, I have the feeling I once read at least one of these books."

"I have the same feeling."

"Tell me about it. I want to read it again and see if I remember anything."

"I can't. But...well, I think I might have once seen you holding a copy of *Little Dorrit*. The Dickens novel."

"I went to Princeton and Cambridge, I know who wrote *Little Dorrit*," she said, irritated. "Wait. Did I ever throw a copy of that book overboard?"

"Might've."

PETER STRAUB

"Why would I do that?"

Ballard shrugged. "To see what would happen?"

"Do you remember that?"

"It's tough to say what I remember. Everything's always different, but it's different *now*. I sort of remember a book, though—a book from this library. *Tono Bungay*. H. G. Wells. Didn't like it much."

"Did you throw it overboard?"

"I might've. Yes, I actually might have." He laughed. "I think I did. I mean, I think I'm throwing it overboard right now, if that makes sense."

"Because you didn't—don't—like it?"

Ballard laughed and put down his knife and fork. Only a few bits of the vegetables and a piece of meat the size of a knuckle sliced in half remained on his plate. "Stop eating and give me your plate." It was almost exactly as empty as his, though Sandrine's plate still had two swirls of the yellow sauce.

"Really?"

"I want to show you something."

Reluctantly, she lowered her utensils and handed him her plate. Ballard scraped the contents of his plate onto hers. He got to his feet and picked up a knife and the plate that had been Sandrine's. "Come out on deck with me."

When she stood up, Sandrine glanced at what she had only briefly and partially perceived as a hint of motion at the top of the room, where for the first time she took in a dun-colored curtain hung two or three feet before the end of the oval. What looked to be a brown or suntanned foot, smaller than a normal adult's and perhaps a bit grubby, was just now vanishing behind the curtain. Before Sandrine had deciphered what she thought she had seen, it was gone.

"Just see a rat?" asked Ballard.

Without intending to assent, Sandrine nodded.

"One was out on deck this morning. Disappeared as soon as I spotted it. Don't worry about it, though. The crew, whoever they are, will get rid of them. At the start of the cruise, I think there are always a few rats around. By the time we really get in gear, they're gone."

"Good," she said, wondering: *If the waiters are these really, really short Indian guys, would they hate us enough to make us eat rats?*

She followed him through the door between the two portholes into pitiless sunlight and crushing

PETER STRAUB

heat made even less comfortable by the dense, invasive humidity. The invisible water saturating the air pressed against her face like a steaming washcloth, and moisture instantly coated her entire body. Leaning against the rail, Ballard looked cool and completely at ease.

"I forgot we had air conditioning," she said.

"We don't. Vents move the air around somehow. Works like magic, even when there's no breeze at all. Come over here."

She joined him at the rail. Fifty yards away, what might have been human faces peered at them through a dense screen of jungle—weeds with thick, vegetal leaves of a green so dark it was nearly black. The half-seen faces resembled masks, empty of feeling.

"Remember saying something about being happy to bathe in the Amazon? About washing your clothes in the river?"

She nodded.

"You never want to go into this river. You don't even want to stick the tip of your finger in that water. Watch what happens, now. Our native friends came out to see this, you should, too."

"The Indians knew you were going to put on this demonstration? How could they?"

"Don't ask me, ask them. *I* don't know how they do it."

Ballard leaned over the railing and used his knife to scrape the few things on the plate into the river. Even before the little knuckles of meat and gristle, the shreds of vegetables, and liquid strings of gravy landed in the water, a six-inch circle of turbulence boiled up on the slow-moving surface. When the bits of food hit the water, the boiling circle widened out into a three-foot, thrashing chaos of violent little fish tails and violent little green shiny fish backs with violent tiny green fins, all in furious motion. The fury lasted about thirty seconds, then disappeared back under the river's sluggish brown face.

"Like Christmas dinner with my husband's family," Sandrine said.

"When we were talking about throwing *Tono Bungay* and *Little Dorrit* into the river to see what would happen—"

"The fish ate the books?"

"They'll eat anything that isn't metal."

"So our little friends don't go swimming all that often, do they?"

PETER STRAUB

"They never learn how. Swimming is death, it's for people like us. Let's go back in, okay?"

She whirled around and struck his chest, hard, with a pointed fist. "I want to go back to the room with the table in it. *Our* table. And this time, you can get as hard as you like."

"Don't I always?" he asked.

"Oh," Sandrine said, "I like that 'always.'"

"And yet, it's always different."

"I bet *I'm* always different," said Sandrine. "You, you'd stay pretty much the same."

"I'm not as boring as all that, you know," Ballard said, and went on, over the course of the long afternoon and sultry evening, to prove it.

After breakfast the next morning, Sandrine, hissing with pain, her skin clouded with bruises, turned on him with such fury that he gasped in joy and anticipation.

{ 1976

*E*nd of November, hot sticky muggy, a vegetal stink in the air. Motionless tribesmen four feet tall stared out from the overgrown bank over twenty yards of torpid river. They held, seemed to hold, bows without arrows, though the details swam backward into the layers of folded green.

"Look at those little savages," said Sandrine Loy, nineteen years old and already contemplating marriage to handsome, absurdly wealthy Antonio Barban, who had proposed to her after a chaotic Christmas dinner at his family's vulgar pile in Greenwich, Connecticut. That she knew marriage to Antonio would prove to be an error of sublime proportions gave the idea most of its appeal. "We're putting on a traveling circus for their benefit. Doesn't that sort of make you detest them?"

"I don't detest them at all," Ballard said. "Actually, I have a lot of respect for those people. I think they're mysterious. So much gravity. So much *silence*. They understand a million things we don't, and what we do manage to get they know about in another way, a more profound way."

"You're wrong. They're too stupid to understand anything. They have mud for dinner. They have mud for brains."

"And yet...." Ballard said, smiling at her.

As if they knew they had been insulted and seemingly without moving out of position, the river people had begun to fade back into the network of dark, rubbery leaves in which they had for a long moment been framed.

"And yet what?"

"They knew what we were going to do. They wanted to see us throwing those books into the river. So out of the bushes they popped, right at the time we walked out on deck."

Her conspicuous black eyebrows slid nearer each other, creating a furrow. She shook her beautiful head and opened her mouth to disagree.

PETER STRAUB

"Anyway, Sandrine, what did you think of what happened just now? Any responses, reflections?"

"What do I think of what happened to the books? What do I think of the fish?"

"Of course," Ballard said. "It's not *all* about us."

He leaned back against the rail, communicating utter ease and confidence. He was forty-four, attired daily in dark tailored suits and white shirts that gleamed like a movie star's smile, the repository of a thousand feral secrets, at home everywhere in the world, the possessor of an understanding it would take him a lifetime to absorb. Sandrine often seemed to him the center of his life. He knew exactly what she was going to say.

"I think the fish are astonishing," she said. "I mean it. Astonishing. Such concentration, such power, such complete *hunger*. It was breathtaking. Those books didn't last more than five or six seconds. All that thrashing! My book lasted longer than yours, but not by much."

"*Little Dorrit* is a lot longer than *Tono Bungay*. More paper, more thread, more glue. I think they're especially hot for glue."

"Maybe they're just hot for Dickens."

"Maybe they're speed readers," said Sandrine. "What do we do now?"

"What we came here to do," Ballard said, and moved back to swing open the dining room door, then froze in mid-step.

"Forget something?"

"I was having the oddest feeling, and I just now realized what it was. You read about it all the time, so you think it must be pretty common, but until a second ago I don't think I'd ever before had the feeling that I was being watched. Not really."

"But now you did."

"Yes." He strode up to the door and swung it open. The table was bare, and the room was empty.

Sandrine approached and peeked over his shoulder. He had both amused and dismayed her. "The great Ballard exhibits a moment of paranoia. I think I've been wrong about you all this time. You're just another boring old creep who wants to fuck me."

"I'd admit to being a lot of things, but paranoid isn't one of them." He gestured her back through the door. That Sandrine obeyed him seemed to take both of them by surprise.

"How about being a boring old creep? I'm not really so sure I want to stay here with you. For one thing, and I know this is not related, the birds keep waking me up. If they are birds."

He cocked his head, interested. "What else could they be? Please tell me. Indulge a boring old creep."

"The maids and the waiters and the sailor guys. The cook. The woman who arranges the flowers."

"You think they belong to that tribe that speaks in bird calls? Actually, how did *you* ever hear about them?"

"My anthropology professor was one of the people who first discovered that tribe. The Pirahas. Know what they call themselves? The tall people. Not very observant are they? According to the professor, they worshipped a much older tribe that had disappeared many generations back— miracle people, healers, shamans, warriors. The Old Ones, they called them, but the Old Ones called themselves **We**, you always have to put it in boldface. My professor couldn't stop talking about these tribes—he was so full of himself. *Soooo* vain. Kept staring at me. Vain, ugly, and lecherous—my favorite trifecta!"

The memory of her anthropology professor, with whom she had clearly gone through the customary adoration-boredom-disgust cycle of student-teacher love affairs, had put Sandrine in a sulky, dissatisfied mood.

"You made a lovely little error about thirty seconds ago. The tribe is called the Piraha, not the Piranhas. Piranhas are the fish you fell in love with."

"Ooh," she said, brightening up. "So the Piraha eat piranhas?"

"Other way around, more likely. But the other people on the *Blinding Light* can't be Piraha, we're hundreds of miles from their territory."

"You *are* tedious. Why did I ever let myself get talked into coming here, anyhow?"

"You fell in love with me the first time you saw me—in your father's living room, remember? And although it was tremendously naughty of me, in fact completely wrong and immoral, I took one look at your stupid sweatshirt and your stupid pigtails and fell in love with you on the spot. You were perfect—you took my breath away. It was like being struck by lightning."

He inhaled, hugely.

"And here I am, thirty-eight years of age, height of my powers, capable of performing miracles on behalf of our clients, exactly as I pulled off,

PETER STRAUB

not to say any more about this, a considerable miracle for your father, plus I am a fabulously eligible
man, a tremendous catch, but what do you know,
still unmarried. Instead of a wife or even a steady
girlfriend, there's this succession of inane young
women from twenty-five to thirty, these Heathers
and Ashleys, these Morgans and Emilys, who
much to their dismay grow less and less infatuated
with me the more time we spend together. 'You're
always so distant,' one of them said, 'you're never
really *with* me.' And she was right, I couldn't really
be with her. Because I wanted to be with you. I
wanted us to be *here*."

Deeply pleased, Sandrine said, "You're such a
pervert."

Yet something in what Ballard had evoked was
making the handsome dining room awkward and
dark. She wished he wouldn't stand still; there
was no reason why he couldn't go into the living
room, or the other way, into the room where terror and fascination beckoned. She wondered why
she was waiting for Ballard to decide where to go,
and as he spoke of seeing her for the first time, was
assailed by an uncomfortably precise echo from
the day in question.

Then, as now, she had been rooted to the floor: in her family's living room, beyond the windows familiar Park Avenue humming with the traffic she only in that moment became aware she heard, Sandrine had been paralyzed. Every inch of her face had turned hot and red. She felt intimate with Ballard before she had even begun to learn what intimacy meant. Before she had left the room, she waited for him to move between herself and her father, then pushed up the sleeves of the baggy sweatshirt and revealed the inscriptions of self-loathing, self-love, desire and despair upon her pale forearms.

"You're pretty weird, too. You'd just had your fifteenth birthday, and here you were, gobsmacked by this old guy in a suit. You even showed me your arms!"

"I could tell what made *you* salivate." She gave him a small, lop-sided smile. "So why were you there, anyhow?"

"Your father and I were having a private cele-bration."

"Of what?"

Every time she asked this question, he gave her a different answer. "I made the fearsome problem

PETER STRAUB

of his old library fines disappear. *Poof!*, no more late-night sweats." Previously, Ballard had told her that he'd got her father off jury duty, had cancelled his parking tickets, retroactively upgraded his B- in Introductory Chemistry to an A.

"Yeah, what a relief. My father never walked into a library, his whole life."

"You can see why the fine was so great." He blinked. "I just had an idea." Ballard wished her to cease wondering, to the extent this was possible, about the service he had rendered for her father. "How would you like to take a peek at the galley? Forbidden fruit, all that kind of thing. Aren't you curious?"

"You're suggesting we go down those stairs? Wasn't *not* doing that one of our most sacred rules?"

"I believe we were given those rules in order to make sure we broke them."

Sandrine considered this proposition for a moment, then nodded her head.

That's my girl, he thought.

"You may be completely perverted, Ballard, but you're pretty smart." A discordant possibility occurred to her. "What if we catch sight of our extremely discreet servants?"

"Then we know for good and all if they're little tribesmen who chirp like bobolinks or handsome South American yacht bums. But that won't happen. They may, in fact they undoubtedly do, see us, but we'll never catch sight of them. No matter how brilliantly we try to outwit them."

"You think they watch us?"

"I'm sure that's one of their main jobs."

"Even when we're in bed? Even when we... you know."

"Especially then," Ballard said.

"What do we think about that, Ballard? Do we love the whole idea, or does it make us sick? You first."

"Neither one. We can't do anything about it, so we might as well forget it. I think being able to watch us is one of the ways they're paid—these tribes don't have much use for money. And because they're always there, they can step in and help us when we need it, at the end."

"So it's like love," said Sandrine.

"Tough love, there at the finish. Let's go over and try the staircase."

"Hold on. When we were out on deck, you told me that you felt you were being watched,

PETER STRAUB

and that it was the first time you'd ever had that feeling."

"Yes, that was different—I don't *feel* the natives watching me, I just assume they're doing it. It's the only way to explain how they can stay out of sight all the time."

As they moved across the dining room to the inner door, for the first time Sandrine noticed a curtain the color of a dark camel hair coat hanging up at the top of the room's oval. Until that moment, she had taken it for a wall too small and oddly shaped to be covered with bookshelves. The curtain shifted a bit, she thought: a tiny ripple occurred in the fabric, as if it had been breathed upon.

There's one of them now, she thought. *I bet they have their own doors and their own staircases.*

For a moment, she was disturbed by a vision of the yacht honeycombed with narrow passages and runways down which beetled small red-brown figures with matted black hair and faces like dull, heavy masks. Now and then the little figures paused to peer through chinks in the walls. It made her feel violated, a little, but at the same time immensely proud of the body that the unseen and

45

silent attendants were privileged to gaze at. The thought of these mysterious little people watching what Ballard did to that body, and she to his, caused a thrill of deep feeling to course upward through her body.

"Stop daydreaming, Sandrine, and get over here." Ballard held the door that led to the gray landing and the metal staircase.

"You go first," she said, and Ballard moved through the frame while still holding the door. As soon as she was through, he stepped around her to grasp the gray metal rail and begin moving down the stairs.

"What makes you so sure the galley's downstairs?"

"Galleys are always downstairs."

"And why do you want to go there, again?"

"One: because they ordered us not to. Two: because I'm curious about what goes on in that kitchen. And three: I also want to get a look at the wine cellar. How can they keep giving us these amazing wines? Remember what we drank with lunch?"

"Some stupid red. It tasted good, though."

"That stupid red was a '55 Chateau Petrus. Two years older than you."

PETER STRAUB

Ballard led her down perhaps another dozen steps, arrived at a landing, and saw one more long staircase leading down to yet another landing.

"How far down can this galley be?" she asked.

"Good question."

"This boat has a bottom, after all."

"It has a hull, yes."

"Shouldn't we actually have gone past it by now? The bottom of the boat?"

"You'd think so. Okay, maybe this is it."

The final stair ended at a gray landing that opened out into a narrow gray corridor leading to what appeared to be a large, empty room. Ballard looked down into the big space, and experienced a violent reluctance, a mental and physical refusal, to go down there and look further into the room: it was prohibited by an actual taboo. That room was not for him, it was none of his business, period. Chilled, he turned from the corridor and at last saw what was directly before him. What had appeared to be a high gray wall was divided in the middle and bore two brass panels at roughly chest height. The wall was a doorway.

"What do you want to do?" Sandrine asked.

Ballard placed a hand on one of the panels and pushed. The door swung open, revealing a white tile floor, metal racks filled with cast-iron pans, steel bowls, and other cooking implements. The light was a low, diffused dimness. Against the side wall, three sinks of varying sizes bulged downward beneath their faucets. He could see the inner edge of a long, shiny metal counter. Far back, a yellow propane tank clung to a range with six burners, two ovens, and a big griddle. A faint mewing, a tiny *skritch skritch skritch* came to him from the depths of the kitchen.

"Look, is there any chance…?" Sandrine whispered.

In a normal voice, Ballard said "No. They're not in here right now, whoever they are. I don't think they are, anyhow."

"So does that mean we're supposed to go inside?"

"How would I know?" He looked over his shoulder at her. "Maybe we're not *supposed* to do anything, and we just decide one way or the other. But here we are, anyhow. I say we go in, right? If it feels wrong, smells wrong, whatever, we boogie on out."

PETER STRAUB

"You first," she said.

Without opening the door any wider, Ballard slipped into the kitchen. Before he was all the way in, he reached back and grasped Sandrine's wrist.

"Come along now."

"You don't have to drag me, I was right behind you. You bully."

"I'm not a bully, I just don't want to be in here by myself."

"All bullies are cowards, too."

She edged in behind him and glanced quickly from side to side. "I didn't think you could have a kitchen like this on a yacht."

"You can't," he said. "Look at that gas range. It must weigh a thousand pounds."

She yanked her wrist out of his hand. "It's hard to see in here, though. Why is the light so fucking weird?"

They were edging away from the door, Sandrine so close behind that Ballard could feel her breath on his neck.

"There aren't any light fixtures, see? No over-head lights, either."

He looked up and saw, far above, only a dim white-gray ceiling that stretched away a great distance on either side. Impossibly, the "galley" seemed much wider than the *Blinding Light* itself.

"I don't like this," he said.

"Me, neither."

"We're really not supposed to be here," he said, thinking of that other vast room down at the end of the corridor, and said to himself, *That's what they call the "engine room," we absolutely can't even glance that way again, can't can't can't, the "engines" would be way too much for us.*

The mewing and skritching, which had momentarily fallen silent, started up again, and in the midst of what felt and tasted to him like panic, Ballard had a vision of a kitten trapped behind a piece of kitchen equipment. He stepped forward and leaned over to peer into the region beyond the long counter and beside the enormous range. Two funny striped cabinets about five feet tall stood there side by side.

"Do you hear a cat?" he asked.

"If you think that's a cat…" Sandrine said, a bit farther behind him than she had been at first.

The cabinets were cages, and what he had seen as stripes were their bars. "Oh," Ballard said, and

PETER STRAUB

sounded as though he had been punched in the stomach.

"Damn you, you started to bleed through your suit jacket," Sandrine whispered. "We have to get out of here, fast."

Ballard scarcely heard her. In any case, if he were bleeding, it was of no consequence. They knew what to do about bleeding. Here, on the other hand, perhaps sixty feet away in this preposterous "galley," was a phenomenon he had never before witnessed. The first cage contained a thrashing beetle-like insect nearly too large for it. This gigantic insect was the source of the mewing and scratching. One of its mandibles rasped at a bar as the creature struggled to roll forward or back, producing noises of insect-distress. Long smeary wounds in the wide middle area between its scrabbling legs oozed a yellow ichor.

Horrified, Ballard looked hastily into the second cage, which he had thought empty but for a roll of blankets, or towels, or the like, and discovered that the blankets or towels were occupied by a small boy from one of the river tribes who was gazing at him through the bars. The boy's eyes looked hopeless and dead. Half of his shoulder seemed to have been sliced away, and a long, thin strip of bone gleamed white against a great scoop of red. The arm half-extended through the bars concluded in a dark, messy stump.

The boy opened his mouth and released, almost too softly to be heard, a single high-pitched musical note. Pure, accurate, well defined, clearly a word charged with some deep emotion, the note hung in the air for a brief moment, underwent a briefer half-life, and was gone.

"What's that?" Sandrine said.

"Let's get out of here."

He pushed her through the door, raced around her, and began charging up the stairs. When they reached the top of the steps and threw themselves into the dining room, Ballard collapsed onto the floor, then rolled onto his back, heaving in great quantities of air. His chest rose and fell, and with every exhalation he moaned. A portion of his left side pulsing with pain felt warm and wet. Sandrine leaned against the wall, breathing heavily in a less convulsive way. After perhaps thirty seconds, she managed to say, "I trust that was a bird down there."

PETER STRAUB

"Um. Yes." He placed his hand on his chest, then held it up like a stop sign, indicating that he would soon have more to say. After a few more great heaving lungfuls of air, he said, "Toucan. In a big cage."

"You were that frightened by a kind of parrot?"

He shook his head slowly from side to side on the polished floor. "I didn't want them to catch us down there. It seemed dangerous, all of a sudden. Sorry."

"You're bleeding all over the floor."

"Can you get me a new bandage pad?"

Sandrine pushed herself off the wall and stepped toward him. From his perspective, she was as tall as a statue. Her eyes glittered. "Screw you, Ballard. I'm not your servant. You can come with me. It's where we're going, anyhow."

He pushed himself upright and peeled off his suit jacket before standing up. The jacket fell to the floor with a squishy thump. With blood-dappled fingers, he unbuttoned his shirt and let that, too, fall to the floor.

"Just leave those things there," Sandrine said. "The invisible crew will take care of them."

"I imagine you're right." Ballard managed to get to his feet without staggering. Slow-moving blood continued to ooze down his left side.

"We have to get you on the table," Sandrine said. "Hold this over the wound for right now, okay?"

She handed him a folded white napkin, and he clamped it over his side. "Sorry. I'm not as good at stitches as you are."

"I'll be fine," Ballard said, and began moving, a bit haltingly, toward the next room.

"Oh, sure. You always are. But you know what I like about what we just did?"

For once he had no idea what she might say. He waited for it.

"That amazing food we loved so much was Toucan! Who would've guessed? You'd think Toucan would taste sort of like chicken, only a lot worse."

"Life is full of surprises."

In the bedroom, Ballard kicked off his shoes, pulled his trousers down over his hips, and stepped out of them.

"You can leave your socks on," said Sandrine, "but let's get your undies off, all right?"

PETER STRAUB

"I need your help."

Sandrine grasped the waistband of his boxers and pulled them down, but they snagged on his penis. "Ballard is aroused, surprise number two." She unhooked his shorts, let them drop to the floor, batted his erection down, and watched it bounce back up. "Barkis is willin', all right."

"Let's get into the workroom," he said.

"Aye aye, *mon capitain.*" Sandrine closed her hand on his erection and said, "Want to go there on-deck, give the natives a look at your magnificent manliness? Shall we increase the index of penis envy among the river tribes by a really big factor?"

"Let's just get in there, okay?"

She pulled him into the workroom and only then released his erection.

A wheeled aluminum tray had been rolled up beside the worktable. Sometimes it was not given to them, and they were forced to do their work with their hands and whatever implements they had brought with them. Today, next to the array of knives of many kinds and sizes, cleavers, wrenches, and hammers lay a pack of surgical thread and a stainless steel needle still warm from the autoclave.

Ballard sat down on the worktable, pushed himself along until his heels had cleared the edge, and lay back. Sandrine threaded the needle and, bending over to get close to the wound, began to do her patient, expert stitching.

PETER STRAUB

{ 1982

O h, here you are," said Sandrine, walking into the sitting room of their suite to find Ballard lying on one of the sofas, reading a book whose title she could not quite make out. Because both of his hands were heavily bandaged, he was having some difficulty turning the pages. "I've been looking all over for you."

He glanced up, frowning. "All over? Does that mean you went down the stairs?"

"No, of course not. I wouldn't do anything like that alone, anyhow."

"And just to make sure.... You didn't go up the stairs, either, did you?"

Sandrine came toward him, shaking her head. "No, I'd never do that, either. But I want to tell you something. I thought *you* might have decided to take a look upstairs. By yourself, to sort of protect me in a way I never want to be protected."

"Of course," Ballard said, closing his book on an index finger that protruded from the bulky white swath of bandage. "You'd hate me if I ever tried to protect you, especially by doing something sneaky. I knew that about you when you were fifteen years old."

"When I was fifteen, you did protect me."

He smiled at her. "I exercised an atypical amount of restraint."

His troublesome client, Sandrine's father, had told him one summer day that a business venture required him to spend a week in Mexico City. Could he think of anything acceptable that might occupy his daughter during that time, she being a teenager a bit too prone to independence and exploration? Let her stay with me, Ballard had said. The guest room has its own bathroom and a TV. I'll take her out to theaters at night, and to the Met and Moma during the day when I'm not doing my job. When I *am* doing my job, she can bat around the city by herself the way she does now. Extraordinary man you are, the client had said, and allow me to reinforce that by letting

PETER STRAUB

you know that about a month ago my daughter just amazed me one morning by telling me that she liked you. You have no idea how god-damned fucking unusual that is. That she talked to me at all is staggering, and that she actually announced that she liked one of my friends is stupefying. So yes, please, thank you, take Sandrine home with you, please do, escort her hither and yon.

When the time came, he drove a compliant Sandrine to his house in Harrison, where he explained that although he would not have sex with her until she was at least eighteen, there were many other ways they could express themselves. And although it would be years before they could be naked together, for the present they would each be able to be naked before the other. Fifteen-year-old Sandrine, who had been expecting to use all her arts of bad temper, insult, duplicity, and evasiveness to escape ravishment by this actually pretty interesting old guy, responded to these conditions with avid interest. Ballard announced another prohibition no less serious, but even more personal.

"I can't cut myself any more?" she asked. "Fuck you, Ballard, you loved it when I showed you my arm. Did my father put you up to this?" She began looking frantically for her bag, which Ballard's valet had already removed to the guest rooms.

"Not at all. Your father would try to kill me if he knew what I was going to do to you. And you to me, when it's your turn."

"So if I can't cut myself, what exactly happens instead?"

"*I* cut you," Ballard said. "And I do it a thousand times better than you ever did. I'll cut you so well no one will ever be able to tell it happened, unless they're right on top of you."

"You think I'll be satisfied with some wimpy little cuts no one can even see? Fuck you all over again."

"Those cuts no one can see will be incredibly painful. And then I'll take the pain away, so you can experience it all over again."

Sandrine found herself abruptly caught up by a rush of feelings that seemed to originate in a deep region located just below her ribcage. At least for the moment, this flood of unnamable emotions blotted out her endless grudges and frustrations, also the chronic bad temper they engendered.

PETER STRAUB

"And during this process, Sandrine, I will become deeply familiar, profoundly familiar with your body, so that when at last we are able to enjoy sex with each other, I will know how to give you the most amazing pleasure. I'll know every inch of you, I'll have your whole gorgeous map in my head. And you will do the same with me."

Sandrine had astonished herself by agreeing to this program on the spot, even to abstain from sex until she turned eighteen. Denial, too, was a pain she could learn to savor. At that point Ballard had taken her upstairs to show her the guest suite, and soon after down the hallway to what he called his "workroom."

"Oh my God," she said, taking it in, "I can't believe it. This is real. And you, you're real, too."

"During the next three years, whenever you start hating everything around you and feel as though you'd like to cut yourself again, remember that I'm here. Remember that this room exists. There'll be many days and nights when we can be here together." In this fashion had Sandrine endured the purgatorial remainder of her days at Dalton. And when she and Ballard at last made love, pleasure and pain had become presences nearly visible in the room at the moment she screamed in the ecstasy of release.

"You dirty, dirty, dirty old man," she said, laughing.

Four years after that, Ballard overheard some Chinese bankers, clients of his firm for whom he had several times rendered his services, speaking in soft Mandarin about a yacht anchored in the Amazon Basin; he needed no more.

"I want to go off the boat for a couple of hours when we get to Manaus," Sandrine said. "I feel like getting back in the world again, at least for a little while. This little private bubble of ours is completely cut off from everything else."

"Which is why—"

"Which is why it works, and why we like it, I understand, but half the time I can't stand it, either. I don't live the way you do, always flying off to interesting places to perform miracles…"

"Try spending a rainy afternoon in Zurich holding some terminally anxious banker's hand."

"Not that it matters, especially, but you don't mind, do you?"

"Of course not. I need some recuperation time, anyhow. This was a little severe." He held

PETER STRAUB

up one thickly bandaged hand. "Not that I'm complaining."

"You'd better not!"

"I'll only complain if you stay out too late— or spend too much of your father's money!"

"What could I buy in Manaus? And I'll make sure to be back before dinner. Have you noticed? The food on this weird boat is getting better and better every day?"

"I know, yes, but for now I seem to have lost my appetite," Ballard said. He had a quick mental vision of a metal cage from which something hideous was struggling to escape. It struck an oddly familiar note, as of something half-remembered, but Ballard was made so uncomfortable by the image in his head that he refused to look at it any longer.

"Will they just know that I want to dock at Manaus?"

"Probably, but you could write them a note. Leave it on the bed. Or on the dining room table."

"I have a pen in my bag, but where can I find some paper?"

"I'd say, look in any drawer. You'll probably find all the paper you might need."

Sandrine went to the little table beside him, pulled open its one drawer and found a single sheet of thick, cream-colored stationery headed *Sweet Delight*. An Omas roller-ball pen, much nicer than the Pilot she had liberated from their hotel in Rio, lay angled atop the sheet of stationery. In her formal, almost italic handwriting, Sandrine wrote *Please dock at Manaus. I would like to spend two or three hours ashore.*

"Should I sign it?"

Ballard shrugged. "There's just the two of us. Initial it."

She drew a graceful, looping S under her note and went into the dining room, where she squared it off in the middle of the table. When she returned to the sitting room, she asked, "And now I just wait? Is that how it works? Just because I found a piece of paper and a pen, I'm supposed to trust this crazy system?"

"You know as much as I do, Sandrine. But I'd say, yes, just wait a little while, yes, that's how it works, and yes, you might as well trust it. There's no reason to be bitchy."

"I have to stay in practice," she said, and lurched sideways as the yacht bumped against something hard and came to an abrupt halt.

PETER STRAUB

"See what I mean?"

When he put the book down in his lap, Sandrine saw that it was *Tono Bungay*. She felt a hot, rapid flare of irritation that the book was not something like *The Women's Room*, which could teach him things he needed to know: and hadn't he already read *Tono Bungay*?

"Look outside, try to catch them tying us up and getting out that walkway thing."

"You think we're in Manaus already?"

"I'm sure we are."

"That's ridiculous. We scraped against a barge or something."

"Nonetheless, we have come to a complete halt."

Sandrine strode briskly to the on-deck door, threw it open, gasped, then stepped outside. The yacht had already been tied up at a long yellow dock at which two yachts smaller than theirs rocked in a desultory brown tide. No crewmen were in sight. The dock led to a wide concrete apron across which men of European descent and a few natives pushed wheelbarrows and consulted clipboards and pulled on cigars while pointing out distant things to other men. It looked false and stagy, like the first scene in a bad musical about New Orleans. An avenue began in front of a row of warehouses, the first of which was painted with the slogan MANAUS AMAZONA. The board walkway with rope handrails had been set in place.

"Yeah, okay," she said. "We really do seem to be docked at Manaus."

"Don't stay away too long."

"I'll stay as long as I like," she said.

The avenue leading past the facades of the warehouses seemed to run directly into the center of the city, visible now to Sandrine as a gathering of tall office buildings and apartment blocks that thrust upwards from the jumble of their surroundings like an outcropping of mountains. The skyscrapers were blue-gray in color, the lower surrounding buildings a scumble of brown, red, and yellow that made Sandrine think of Cezanne, even of Seurat: dots of color that suggested walls and roofs. She thought she could walk to the center of the city in no more than forty-five minutes, which left her about two hours to do some exploring and have lunch.

Nearly an hour later, Sandrine trudged past the crumbling buildings and broken windows on

PETER STRAUB

crazed, tilting sidewalks under a domineering sun. Sweat ran down her forehead and cheeks and plastered her dress to her body. The air seemed half water, and her lungs strained to draw in oxygen. The office buildings did not seem any nearer than at the start of her walk. If she had seen a taxi, she would have taken it back to the port, but only a few cars and pickups rolled along the broad avenue. The dark, half-visible men driving these vehicles generally leaned over their steering wheels and stared at her, as if women were rare in Manaus. She wished she had thought to cover her hair, and was sorry she had left her sunglasses behind.

Then she became aware that a number of men were following her, how many she could not tell, but more than two. They spoke to each other in low, hoarse voices, now and then laughing at some remark sure to be at Sandrine's expense. Although her feet had begun to hurt, she began moving more quickly. Behind her, the men kept pace with her, neither gaining nor falling back. After another two blocks, Sandrine gave in to her sense of alarm and glanced over her shoulder. Four men in dark hats and shapeless, slept-in suits had ranged themselves across the width of the sidewalk. One of them called out to her in a language she did not understand; another emitted a wet, mushy laugh. The man at the curb jumped down into the street, trotted across the empty avenue, and picked up his pace on the sidewalk opposite until he had drawn a little ahead of Sandrine.

She felt utterly alone and endangered. And because she felt in danger, a scorching anger blazed up within her: at herself for so stupidly putting herself at risk, at the men behind her for making her feel frightened, for ganging up on her. She did not know what she was going to have to do, but she was not going to let those creeps get any closer to her than they were now. Twisting to her right, then to her left, Sandrine removed her shoes and rammed them into her bag. They were watching her, the river scum; even the man on the other side of the avenue had stopped moving and was staring at her from beneath the brim of his hat.

Literally testing the literal ground, Sandrine walked a few paces over the paving stones, discovered that they were at any rate not likely to cut her feet, gathered herself within, and, like a race horse bursting from the gate, instantly began running

PETER STRAUB

as fast as she could. After a moment in which her pursuers were paralyzed with surprise, they too began to run. The man on the other side of the street jumped down from the curb and began sprinting toward her. His shoes made a sharp *tick-tick* sound when they met the stony asphalt. As the ticks grew louder, Sandrine heard him inhaling great quantities of air. Before he could reach her, she came to a cross street and wheeled in, her bag bouncing at her hip, her legs stretching out to devour yard after yard of stony ground.

Unknowingly, she had entered a slum. The structures on both sides of the street were half-collapsed huts and shanties made of mismatched wooden planks, of metal sheeting, and tarpaper. She glimpsed faces peering out of greasy windows and sagging, cracked-open doors. Some of the shanties before her were shops with soft drink cans and bottles of beer arrayed on the window sills. People were spilling from little tarpaper and sheet-metal structures out into the street, already congested with abandoned cars, pedestrians, empty pushcarts, and cartons of fruit for sale. Garbage lay everywhere. The women who watched Sandrine streak by displayed no interest in her plight.

Yet the slum's chaos was a blessing, Sandrine thought: the deeper she went, the greater the number of tiny narrow streets sprouting off the one she had taken from the avenue. It was a feverish, crowded warren, a *favela*, the kind of place you would never escape had you the bad luck to have been born there. And while outside this rat's nest the lead man chasing her had been getting dangerously near, within its boundaries the knots of people and the obstacles of cars and carts and mounds of garbage had slowed him down. Sandrine found that she could dodge all of these obstacles with relative ease. The next time she spun around a corner, feet skidding on a slick pad of rotting vegetables, she saw what looked to her like a miracle: an open door revealing a hunched old woman draped in black rags, beckoning her in.

Sandrine bent her legs, called on her youth and strength, jumped off the ground, and sailed through the open door. The old woman only just got out of the way in time to avoid being knocked down. She was giggling, either at Sandrine's athleticism or because she had rescued her from the pursuing thugs. When Sandrine had cleared her dooorway and was scrambling to avoid ramming

PETER STRAUB

into the wall, the old woman darted forward and slammed her door shut. Sandrine fell to her knees in a small room suddenly gone very dark. A slanting shaft of light split the murk and illuminated a rectangular space on the floor covered by a threadbare rug no longer of any identifiable color. Under the light, the rug seemed at once utterly worthless and extraordinarily beautiful.

The old woman shuffled into the shaft of light and uttered an incomprehensible word that sounded neither Spanish nor Portuguese. A thousand wayward wrinkles like knife cuts, scars, and stitches had been etched into her white, elongated face. Her nose had a prominent hook, and her eyes shone like dark stones at the bottom of a fast, clear stream. Then she laid an upright index finger against her sunken lips and with her other hand gestured toward the door. Sandrine listened. In seconds, multiple footsteps pounded past the old woman's little house. Leading the pack was *tick tick tick*. The footsteps clattered up the narrow street and disappeared into the ordinary clamor.

Hunched over almost parallel to the ground, the old woman mimed hysterical laughter. Sandrine mouthed *Thank you, thank you*, thinking that her intention would be clear if the words were not. Still mock-laughing, her unknown savior shuffled closer, knitting and folding her long, spotted hands. She had the ugliest hands Sandrine had ever seen, knobbly arthritic fingers with filthy, ragged nails. She hoped the woman was not going to stroke her hair or pat her face: she would have to let her do it, however nauseated she might feel. Instead, the old woman moved right past her, muttering what sounded like *Munna, munna, num.*

Outside on the street, the ticking footsteps once again became audible. Someone began knocking, hard, on an adjacent door.

Only half-visible at the rear of the room, the old woman turned toward Sandrine and beckoned her forward with an urgent gesture of her bony hand. Sandrine moved toward her, uncertain of what was going on.

In an urgent, raspy whisper: *Munna! Num!*

The old woman appeared to be bowing to the baffled Sandrine, whose sense of peril had begun again to boil up within her. A pane of greater darkness slid open behind the old woman, and Sandrine finally understood that her savior had merely bent herself more deeply to turn a doorknob.

PETER STRAUB

Num! Num!

Sandrine obeyed orders and *nummed* past her beckoning hostess. Almost instantly, instead of solid ground, her foot met a vacancy, and she nearly tumbled down what she finally understood to be a staircase. Only her sense of balance kept her upright: she was grateful she still had all of her crucial toes. Behind her, the door slammed shut. A moment later, she heard the clicking of a lock.

BACK ON THE YACHT, Ballard slipped a bookmark into *Tono Bungay* and for the first time, at least for what he thought was the first time, regarded the pair of red lacquered cabinets against the wall beside him. Previously, he had taken them in, but never really examined them. About four feet high and three feet wide, they appeared to be Chinese and were perhaps moderately valuable. Brass fittings with latch pins held them closed in front, so they were easily opened.

The thought of lifting the pins and opening the cabinets aroused both curiosity and an odd dread in Ballard. For a moment, he had a vision of a great and forbidden room deep in the bowels of the yacht where enormous spiders ranged across rotting, heaped-up corpses. (With wildly variant details, visions of exactly this sort had visited Ballard ever since his adolescence.) He shook his head to clear it of this vision, and when that failed, struck his bandaged left hand against the padded arm of the sofa. Bright, rolling waves of pain forced a gasp from him, and the forbidden room with its spiders and corpses zipped right back to wherever had given it birth.

Was this the sort of dread he was supposed to obey, or the sort he was supposed to ignore? Or if not ignore, because that was always unwise and in some sense dishonorable, acknowledge but persist in the face of anyway? Cradling his throbbing hand against his chest, Ballard let the book slip off his lap and got to his feet, eyeing the pair of shiny cabinets. If asked to inventory the contents of the sitting room, he would have forgotten to list them. Presumably that meant he was supposed to overlook his foreboding and investigate the contents of these vertical little Chinese chests. *They* wanted him to open the cabinets, if *he* wanted to.

PETER STRAUB

Still holding his electrocuted left hand to his chest, Ballard leaned over and brought his exposed right index finger in contact with the box on the left. No heat came from it, and no motion. It did not hum, it did not quiver, however delicately. At least six or seven coats of lacquer had been applied to the thing—he felt as though he were looking into a deep river of red lacquer.

Ballard hunkered and used his index finger to push the brass latch pin up and out of the ornate little lock. It swung down on an intricate little cord he had not previously noticed. The door did not open by itself, as he had hoped. Once again, he had to make a choice, for it was not too late to drop the brass pin back into its latch. He could choose not to look; he could let the *Sweet Delight* keep its secrets. But as before, Ballard acknowledged the dread he was feeling, then dropped his hip to the floor, reached out, and flicked the door open with his fingernail. Arrayed on the cabinet's three shelves were what appeared to be photographs in neat stacks. Polaroids, he thought. He took the first stack of photos from the cabinet and looked down at the topmost one. What Ballard saw there had two contradictory effects on him. He became so light-headed he feared he might faint; and he almost ejaculated into his trousers.

TAKING CARE NOT TO tumble, Sandrine moved in the darkness back to the top of the staircase, found the door with her fingertips, and pounded. The door rattled in its frame but did not give. "Open up, lady!" she shouted. "Are you *kidding*? Open this door!" She banged her fists against the unmoving wood, thinking that although the old woman undoubtedly did not speak English, she could hardly misunderstand what Sandrine was saying. When her fists began to hurt and her throat felt ragged, the strangeness of what had just happened opened before her: it was like… like a fairy tale! She had been duped, tricked, flummoxed; she had been trapped. The world had closed on her, as a steel trap snaps shut on the leg of a bear.

"Please!" she yelled, knowing it was useless. She would not be able to beg her way out of this confinement. Here, the Golden Shower of Shit did

PETER STRAUB

not apply. "Please let me out!" A few more bangs of her fist, a few more shouted pleas to be set free, to be *let go, released.* She thought she heard her ancient captor chuckling to herself.

Two possibilities occurred to her: that her pursuers had driven her to this place and the old woman was in league with them; and that they had not and she was not. The worse by far of these options was the second, that to escape her rapists she had fled into a psychopath's dungeon. Maybe the old woman wanted to starve her to death. Maybe she wanted to soften her up so she'd be easy to kill. Or maybe she was just keeping her as a snack for some monstrous get of hers, some over-grown looney-tunes son with pinwheel eyes and horrible teeth and a vast appetite for stray women.

More to exhaust all of her possibilities than because she imagined they possessed any actual substance, Sandrine turned carefully around, plant-ed a hand on the earthen wall beside her, and began making her way down the stairs in the dark. It would lead to some spider-infested cellar, she knew, a foul-smelling hole where ugly, discarded things waited thug-like in the seamless dark to inflict injury upon anyone who entered their realm.

She would grope her way from wall to wall, feeling for another door, for a high window, for any means to escape, knowing all the while that earthen cellars in shabby slum dwellings never had separate exits.

Five steps down, it occurred to Sandrine that she might not have been the first woman to be locked into this awful basement, and that instead of broken chairs and worn-out tools she might find herself knocking against a ribcage or two, a couple of femurs, that her foot might land on the jawbone, that she might step on somebody's forehead! Her body of a sudden shook, and her mind went white, and for a few moments Sandrine was on the verge of coming unglued: she pictured herself drawn up into a fetal ball, shuddering, weeping, whimpering. For a moment this dreadful image seemed unbearably tempting.

Then she thought, *Why the FUCK isn't Ballard here?*

Ballard was one hell of a tricky dude, he was full of little surprises, you could never really predict what he'd feel like doing, and he was a brilliant problem-solver. That's what Ballard did for a living, he flew around the world mopping up other people's

PETER STRAUB

messes. The only reason Sandrine knew him at all
was that Ballard had materialized in a New Jersey
motel room where good old Dad, Lauritzen Loy,
had been dithering over the corpse of a slaughtered
whore, then caused the whore to vanish, the bloody
sheets to vanish, and for all she knew the motel to
vanish also. Two hours later a shaken but sober
Lauritzen Loy reported to work in an immaculate
and spotless Armani suit and Brioni tie. (Sandrine
had known the details of her father's vile little
peccadillo for years.) Also, and this quality meant
that his presence would have been particularly
valuable down in the witch-hag's cellar, although
Ballard might have looked as though he had never
picked up anything heavier than a briefcase, he was
in fact astonishingly strong, fast, and smart. If you
were experiencing a little difficulty with a dragon,
Ballard was the man for you.

While meditating upon the all-round excellence
of her longtime lover and wishing for him more
with every fresh development of her thought,
Sandrine had been continuing steadily on her
way down the stairs. When she reached the part
about the dragon, it came to her that she had been
on these earthen stairs far longer than she had

expected. Sandrine thought she was now actually beneath the level of the cellar she had expected to enter. The fairy tale feeling came over her again, of being held captive in a world without rational rules and orders, subject to deep patterns unknown to or rejected in the daylit world. In a flash of insight, it came to her that this fairy tale world had much in common with her childhood.

To regain control of herself, perhaps most of all to shake off the sense of gloom-laden helplessness evoked by thoughts of childhood, Sandrine began to count the steps as she descended. Down into the earth they went, the dry firm steps that met her feet, twenty more, then forty, then fifty. At a hundred and one, she felt light-headed and weary, and sat down in the darkness. She felt like weeping. The long stairs were a grave, leading nowhere but to itself. Hope, joy, and desire had fled; even boredom and petulance had fled; hunger, lust, and anger were no more. She felt tired and empty. Sandrine leaned a shoulder against the earthen wall, shuddered once, and realized she was crying only a moment before she fled into unconsciousness.

In that same instant she passed into an ongoing dream, as if she had wandered into the middle

PETER STRAUB

of a story, more accurately a point far closer to its ending. Much, maybe nearly everything of interest, had already happened. Sandrine lay on a mess of filthy blankets at the bottom of a cage. The Golden Shower of Shit had sufficiently relaxed, it seemed, as to permit the butchering of entire slabs of flesh from her body, for much of the meat from her right shoulder had been sliced away. The wound reported a dull, wavering ache that spoke of those wonderful objects, Ballard's narcotic painkillers. So close together were the narrow bars, she could extend only a hand, a wrist, an arm. In her case, an arm, a wrist, and a stump. The hand was absent from the arm Sandrine had slipped through the bars, and someone had cauterized the wounded wrist.

The Mystery of the Missing Hand led directly to Cage Number One, where a giant bug-creature sat crammed in at an angle, filling nearly the whole of the cage, mewing softly, and trying to saw through the bars with its remaining mandible. It had broken the left one on the bars, but it was not giving up, it was a bug, and bugs don't quit. Sandrine was all but certain that when in possession of both mandibles, that is to say before capture, this huge *thing* had used them to saw off her hand, which it had then promptly devoured. The giant bugs were the scourge of the river tribes. However, the Old Ones, the Real People, the Cloud Huggers, the Tree Spirits, the archaic Sacred Ones who spoke in birdsong and called themselves **We** had so shaped the River and the Forest, which had given them birth, that the meat of the giant bugs tasted exceptionally good, and a giant bug guilty of eating a person or parts of a person became by that act overwhelmingly delicious, like manna, like the food of paradise for human beings. **We** were feeding bits of Sandrine to the captured bug that it might yield stupendous meals for the Sandrine and Ballard upstairs.

Sandrine awakened crying out in fear and horror, scattering tears she could not see.

Enough of that. Yes, quite enough of quivering; it was time to decide what to do next. Go back and try to break down the door, or keep going down and see what happens? Sandrine hated the idea of giving up and going backwards. She levered herself upright and resumed her descent with stair number one hundred and two.

PETER STRAUB

At stair three hundred she passed through another spasm of weepy trembling, but soon conquered it and moved on. By the four hundredth stair she was hearing faint carnival music and seeing sparkly light-figments flit through the darkness like illuminated moths. Somewhere around stair five hundred she realized that the numbers had become mixed up in her head, and stopped counting. She saw a grave that wasn't a grave, merely darkness, and she saw her old tutor at Clare, a cool, detached Don named Quentin Jester who said things like, "If I had a lifetime with you, Miss Loy, we'd both know a deal more than we do at present," but she closed her eyes and shook her head and sent him packing.

Many stairs later, Sandrine's thigh muscles reported serious aches, and her arms felt extraordinarily heavy. So did her head, which kept lolling forward to rest on her chest. Her stomach complained, and she said to herself, *Wish I had a nice big slice of sautéed giant bug right about now,* and chuckled at how crazy she had become in so short a time. Giant bug! Even good old Dad, old LL, who often respected sanity in others but wished for none of it himself, drew the line at dining on giant insects. And here came yet another proof of her deteriorating mental condition, that despite her steady progress deeper and deeper underground, Sandrine could almost sort of half-persuade herself that the darkness before her seemed weirdly less dark than only a moment ago. This lunatic delusion clung to her step after step, worsening as she went. She said to herself, I'll hold up my hand, and if I think I see it, I'll know it's good-bye, real world, pack Old Tillie off to Bedlam. She stopped moving, closed her eyes, and raised her hand before her face. Slowly, she opened her eyes, and beheld...her hand!

The problem with the insanity defense lay in the irrevocable truth that it was really her hand before her, not a mad vision from Gothic literature but her actual, entirely earthly hand, at present grimy and crusted with dirt from its long contact with the wall. Sandrine turned her head and discovered that she could make out the wall, too, with its hard-packed earth showing here and there the pale string of a severed root, at times sending in her direction a little spray or shower of dusty particulate. Sandrine held her breath and looked down to what appeared to be the source of the illumination. Then she inhaled sharply, for it seemed to her that she could see, dimly and a long way down, the bottom of the stairs. A little rectangle of light burned away down there, and from it floated the luminous translucency that made it possible for her to see.

Too shocked to cry, too relieved to insist on its impossibility, Sandrine moved slowly down the remaining steps to the rectangle of light. Its warmth heated the air, the steps, the walls, and Sandrine herself, who only now registered that for most of her journey she had been half-paralyzed by the chill leaking from the earth. As she drew nearer to the light, she could finally make out details of what lay beneath her. She thought she saw a strip of concrete, part of a wooden barrel, the bottom of a ladder lying on the ground: the intensity of the light surrounding these enigmatic objects shrank and dwindled them, hollowed them out even as it drilled painfully into her eyes. Beneath her world existed another, its light a blinding dazzle.

When Sandrine had come within thirty feet of the blazing underworld, her physical relationship to it mysteriously altered. It seemed she no longer stepped downward, but moved across a slanting plane that leveled almost imperceptibly off. The dirt walls on either side fell back and melted to ghostly gray air, to nothing solid, until all that remained was the residue of dust and grime plastered over Sandrine's white dress, her hands and face, her hair. Heat reached her, the real heat of an incendiary sun, and human voices, and the clang and bang and underlying susurrus of machinery. She walked toward all of it, shading her eyes as she went.

Through the simple opening before her Sandrine moved, and the sun blazed down upon her, and her own moisture instantly soaked her filthy dress, and sweat turned the dirt in her hair to muddy trickles. She knew this place; the dazzling underworld was the world she had left. From beneath her shading hand Sandrine took in the wide concrete apron, the equipment she had noticed all that harrowing time ago and the equipment she had not, the men posturing for the benefit of other men, the sense of falsity and stagecraft and the incipient swelling of a banal unheard melody. The long yellow dock where on a sluggish umber tide three yachts slowly rocked, one of them the *Sweet Delight*.

PETER STRAUB

The Ballad of BALLARD AND SANDRINE

In a warm breeze that was not a breeze, a soiled-looking scrap of paper flipped toward Sandrine over the concrete, at the last lifting off the ground to adhere to her leg. She bent down to peel it off and release it, and caught a strong, bitter whiff, unmistakably excremental, of the Amazon. The piece of paper wished to cling to her leg, and there it hung until the second tug of Sandrine's dirty fingers, when she observed that she was gripping not a scrap of paper but a Polaroid, now a little besmudged by contact with her leg. When she raised it to her face, runnels of dirt obscured portions of the image. She brushed away much of the dirt, but could still make no sense of the photograph, which appeared to depict some pig-like animal.

In consternation, she glanced to one side and found there, lounging against bollards and aping the idleness of degenerates and river louts, two of the men in shabby suits and worn-out hats who had pursued her into the slum. She straightened up in rage and terror, and to confirm what she already knew to be the case, looked to her other side and saw their companions. One of them waved to her. Sandrine's terror cooled before her perception that these guys had changed in some basic way. Maybe they weren't idle, exactly, but these men were more relaxed, less predatory than they had been on the avenue into Manaus.

They had their eyes on her, though, they were interested in what she was going to do. Then she finally got it: they were different because now she was where they had wanted her to be all along. They didn't think she would try to escape again, but they wanted to make sure. Sandrine's whole long adventure, from the moment she noticed she was being followed to the present, had been designed to funnel her back to the dock and the yacht. The four men, who were now smiling at her and nodding their behatted heads, had pushed her toward the witch-hag, for they were all in it together! Sandrine dropped her arms, took a step backward, and in amazement looked from side to side, taking in all of them. It had all been a trick; herded like a cow, she had been played. Falsity again; more stagecraft.

One of the nodding, smiling men held his palm up before his face, and the man beside him leaned forward and laughed into his fist, as if shielding a sneeze. Grinning at her, the first man went through

PETER STRAUB

his meaningless mime act once again, lifting his left hand and staring into its palm. Grinning even more widely, he pointed at Sandrine and shouted, "*Munna!*"

The man beside him cracked up, *Munna!*, what a wit, then whistled an odd little four note melody that might have been a birdcall.

Experimentally, Sandrine raised her left hand, regarded it, and realized that she was still gripping the dirty little Polaroid photograph of a pig. Those two idiots off to her left waved their hands in ecstasy. She was doing the right thing, so *Munna!* right back atcha, buddy. She looked more closely at the Polaroid and saw that what it pictured was not actually a pig. The creature in the photo had a head and a torso, but little else. The eyes, nose, and ears were gone. A congeries of scars like punctuation marks, like snakes, like words in an unknown language, decorated the torso.

I know what Munna *means, and* Num, thought Sandrine, and for a moment experienced a spasm of stunning, utterly sexual warmth before she fully understood what had been given her: that she recognized the man in the photo. The roar of oceans, of storm-battered leaves, filled her ears and caused her head to spin and wobble. Her fingers parted, and the Polaroid floated off in an artificial, wind-machine breeze that spun it around a couple of times before lifting it high above the port and winking it out of sight, lost in the bright hard blue above the *Sweet Delight*.

Sandrine found herself moving down the yellow length of the long dock.

Tough love, Ballard had said. To be given and received, at the end perfectly repaid by that which she had perhaps glimpsed but never witnessed, the brutal, exalted, slow-moving force that had sometimes rustled a curtain, sometimes moved through this woman, her hair and body now dark with mud, had touched her between her legs, Sandrine, poor profane lost deluded most marvelously fated Sandrine.

PETER STRAUB

{ 1997

From the galley they come, from behind the little dun-colored curtain in the dining room, from behind the bookcases in the handsome sitting room, from beneath the bed and the bloodstained metal table, through wood and fabric and the weight of years, **We** come, the Old Ones and Real People, the Cloud Huggers, **We** process slowly toward the center of the mystery **We** understand only by giving it unquestioning service. What remains of the clients and patrons lies, still breathing though without depth or force, upon the metal work-table. It was always going to end this way, it always does, it can no other. Speaking in the high-pitched, musical language of birds that **We** taught the Piraha at the beginning of time, **We** gather at the site of these ruined bodies, **We** worship their devotion to each other and the Great Task that grew and will grow on them, **We** treat them with grave tenderness as **We** separate what can and must be separated. Notes of the utmost liquid purity float upward from the mouths of **We** and print themselves upon the air. **We** know what they mean, though they have long since passed through the realm of words and gained again the transparency of music. **We** love and accept the weight and the weightlessness of music. When the process of separation is complete, through the old sacred inner channels **We** transport what the dear, still-living man and woman have each taken from the other's body down down down to the galley and the ravening hunger that burns ever within it.

Then. Then. With the utmost tenderness, singing the deep tuneless music at the heart of the ancient world, **We** gather up what remains of Ballard and Sandrine, armless and legless trunks, faces without features, their breath clinging to their mouths like wisps, carry them (in our arms, in baskets, in once-pristine sheets) across the deck and permit them to roll from our care, as they had always longed to do, and into that of the flashing furious little river-monarchs. **We** watch the water

PETER STRAUB

boil in a magnificence of ecstasy, and **We** sing for as long as it lasts.